★ CONTENTS ★

Over the Stile
and into the Sack

Retold by *Rose Impey*

Illustrated by *Hilda Offen*

ORCHARD BOOKS

Other titles in this series:

Bad Bears and Good Bears

Bad Boys and Naughty Girls

Greedy Guts and Belly Busters

Hairy Toes and Scary Bones

I Spy, Pancakes and Pies

If Wishes were Fishes

Knock, Knock! Who's There?

Runaway Cakes and Skipalong Pots

Silly Sons and Dozy Daughters

Sneaky Deals and Tricky Tricks

Ugly Dogs and Slimy Frogs

ORCHARD BOOKS
96 Leonard Street, London EC2A 4XD
Orchard Books Australia
14 Mars Road, Lane Cove, NSW 2066
First published in Great Britain in 2000
First paperback publication 2000
Text © Rose Impey 2000
Illustrations © Hilda Offen 2000
The rights of Rose Impey to be identified as the author
and Hilda Offen as the illustrator of this work
have been asserted by them in accordance with the
Copyright, Designs and Patents Act, 1988.
A CIP catalogue record for this book is available
from the British Library.
ISBN 1 86039 975 4 (hardback)
ISBN 1 86039 976 2 (paperback)
1 3 5 7 9 10 8 6 4 2 (hardback)
1 3 5 7 9 10 8 6 4 2 (paperback)
Printed in Great Britain

Mr Fox
★ and His Sack ★

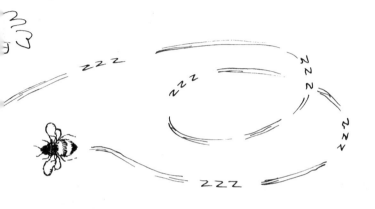

One day Mr Fox was digging
near a tree when he found a
buzzy-buzzy bee.

He grabbed the bee and popped
it in his sack. Then he set off
down the road, *pit, pat, pitter-pat*
on his neat little feet.

He came to a tall thin house with a tall thin woman at the door.

"Good morning," said Mr Fox.
"May I leave my sack with you
while I go to Squantum's house?"

"You may," said the tall thin
woman.

"Be careful," said Mr Fox.
"Don't open it, whatever you do."

And off he went, *pit, pat,*
pitter-pat on his neat little feet
to Squantum's house.

But the moment he'd gone what do you think she did? She opened the sack and out flew the bee, *buzz, buzz, buzzy-buzz,* and her cock-a-doodle-doo caught it and gobbled it up.

Soon Mr Fox came back.
Uh-oh! He could smell trouble.

"Where's my buzzy-buzzy bee?"
he said.

"I just *peeped* inside," said the tall thin woman, "but the bee flew out and my doodle-doo ate it up."

"Then I'll take your doodle-doo instead," said Mr Fox. And he put it in his sack and set off down the road.

He came to a little round house
with a little round woman at the
door.

"Good morning," said Mr Fox.
"Can I leave my sack with you
while I go to Squintum's house?"
"You certainly can," said the
little round woman.

"Be careful," said Mr Fox.
"Don't open it, whatever you do."

Then off he went, *pit, pat,*
pitter-pat on his neat little feet to
Squintum's house. But as soon as
he'd gone the little round woman
did open it. Just for a peep.

Too late! Out flew the doodle-
doo and her pig gobbled it up.
Just like that!

When Mr Fox came back he could *smell* trouble, and he could *see* it. The sack was empty.

"Where's my doodle-doo?" he cried.

"Oh dear, I just peeped inside," said the little round woman. "The doodle-doo flew out and my pig gobbled it up."

"Then I'll take your pig instead," said Mr Fox. And he put it in his sack and set off down the road.

He came to a twirly-whirly house with a twirly-whirly woman at the door.

"Good morning," said Mr Fox.
"May I leave my sack with you
while I go to Squeeentum's house?"

"With pleasure," said the twirly-
whirly woman.

"Be careful," said Mr Fox.
"Don't open it, whatever you do."

And he set off, *pit*, *pat*, *pitter-pat* on his neat little feet to Squeeentum's house. But the moment he'd gone the twirly-whirly woman *did* open it!

Out jumped the pig and trotted straight through the door.

The woman's little boy chased the pig down the road and across the fields.

When Mr Fox came back he
knew something was wrong.

"Where's my pig?" he cried.

"I just peeped in for a moment,"
cried the twirly-whirly woman,
"but the pig jumped out. My boy
chased it down the road and it
hasn't come back."

"Then I'll take your boy instead," said Mr Fox. And he popped him in his sack and set off down the road.

He came to a rosy-cosy cottage. Standing at the door was a rosy-cosy woman with four rosy-cosy children and their big brown dog.

"Good morning," said Mr Fox.
"Can I leave my sack with you
while I go to Squooontum's house?"

"Of course," said the
rosy-cosy woman.

"Be careful," said Mr Fox.
"Don't open my sack."

Then he set off, *pit, pat, pitter-pat* on his neat little feet to Squooontum's house. After he'd gone the rosy-cosy woman took her children inside for tea.

A big tray of muffins had just finished cooking. They smelled *de-e-e-licious*.

"I want one!" shouted one of the children.

"And me!"
"And me!"
"And me!"
shouted the others.

Then a voice from the sack called out, "Leave one for me."

"My goodness, what's this?" said the rosy-cosy woman. She opened up the sack and let the little boy out.

He sat with the children and ate muffins and when he'd had enough the woman hid him in a cupboard. Then she put the big brown dog in the sack in his place.

When Mr Fox came back there
was such a strong smell of muffins,
he couldn't smell trouble.

And he couldn't see it either; the
sack was still full. So he picked it
up and set off home.

But the smell of muffins had made him feel so hungry he couldn't wait until he got home. He stopped by the side of the road and opened the sack.

When he reached inside though, he didn't find a little boy, he found a big brown dog with long teeth and sharp claws. What a fight there was!

At last Mr Fox ran off on his neat little feet and the big brown dog ran home to the rosy-cosy house. And I hope there was still a muffin left for him when he got there!

Squantum, Squintum,
Squeeentum, Squeee,
Mr Fox caught a
buzzy-buzzy bee,
But the twirly-whirly boy
got free.

The Old Woman and Her Pig

There was once an old woman who was sweeping her house when she found a little silver sixpence.

She set off at once for the market
where she bought a smooth-coated,
black-spotted, curly-tailed pig.

On the way home they came
to a stile, but the piggy wouldn't
go over it.

Along came a dog. So the old
woman said,

"*Dog! Dog! Bite pig!*
Piggy won't go over the stile
and I shall never get home tonight."

But the dog wouldn't bite the
pig. The pig had never hurt him.

Near by was a stick. So the old woman said,

"Stick! Stick! Beat dog!
Dog won't bite pig;
piggy won't go over the stile
and I shall never get home tonight."

But the stick could not, would not beat the dog. The dog had never harmed it.

In the field was a fire. So the old woman said,

"Fire! Fire! Burn stick!

Stick won't beat dog;
dog won't bite pig;
piggy won't go over the stile
and I shall never get home tonight."

But the fire wouldn't do it.

In the same field was a stretch of water. So the old woman said,

"Water! Water! Quench fire!

Fire won't burn stick;
stick won't beat dog;
dog won't bite pig;
piggy won't go over the stile
and I shall never get home tonight."

But do you think the water cared?
Not a bit.

By now the old woman was getting cross. Close by was a cow eating grass, so she said,

"Cow! Cow! Drink water!

Water won't quench fire;
fire won't burn stick;
stick won't beat dog;
dog won't bite pig;
piggy won't go over the stile
and I shall never get home tonight."

But the cow didn't want to
drink; it wasn't thirsty, thank you
very much.

Along came a butcher. The old woman was so cross now she said,

"Butcher! Butcher! Kill cow!

Cow won't drink water;
water won't quench fire;
fire won't burn stick;
stick won't beat dog;
dog won't bite pig;
piggy won't go over the stile
and I shall never get home tonight."

The butcher said, No! no! no!
he wouldn't; the cow had never
hurt him.

Then the old woman spotted a rope hanging from a tree.

"Rope! Rope!" she called.
"Tie this butcher!

Butcher won't kill cow;
cow won't drink water;
water won't quench fire;
fire won't burn stick;
stick won't beat dog;
dog won't bite pig;
piggy won't go over the stile
and I shall never get home tonight."

But the rope was no help at all.
It just hung there.

"Useless," said the old woman.

The next to come along was a
rat. So the old woman said,

"Rat! Rat! Chew rope!

Rope won't tie butcher;
butcher won't kill cow;
cow won't drink water;
water won't quench fire;
fire won't burn stick;
stick won't beat dog;
dog won't bite pig;
piggy won't go over the stile
and I shall never get home tonight."

But a rat is a rat, he wouldn't put himself out. The rope was nothing to him.

The poor old woman was at her wits' end. But then along came a cat. Just the right kind: not a fat, curl-up-on-the-mat cat, but a sleek, chaser-of-rats cat.

"Oh, cat! Kind cat!" said the old woman. *"Please chase rat.*

Rat won't chew rope;
rope won't tie butcher;
butcher won't kill cow;
cow won't drink water;
water won't quench fire;
fire won't burn stick;
stick won't beat dog;
dog won't bite pig;
piggy won't go over the stile
and I shall never get home tonight."

The helpful, *hungry* cat didn't need asking twice. He sharpened his claws, and he stretched his jaws, and then he...pounced.

But the moment he began to chase the rat,

the rat began to
chew the rope;

the rope began to
tie the butcher;

the butcher began to
kill the cow;

the cow began to
drink the water;

the water began to
quench the fire;

the fire began to
burn the stick;

the stick began to
beat the dog;

the dog began to
bite the pig...

...but the smooth-coated, black-spotted, curly-tailed piggy didn't want to be bitten. So...

...he took one leap and jumped over the stile.

When the dog bit the pig,
the pig took fright,
And the little old woman
got home that night.

Many folk tales are made up of a chain of events where things come to a climax when the chain is broken, like the American story *Mr Fox and His Sack*. In others, like *The Old Woman and Her Pig*, one character causes a chain reaction which reverses everything which has happened so far.

Here are some more stories you might like to read:

About Sacks:

The Singing Sack
by Helen East
(A&C Black)

The Cock, The Mouse and The Little Red Hen
from *The Orchard Book of Nursery Stories*
by Sophie Windham
(Orchard Books)

About Chain Reactions:

Anansi and the Pig
from *Nursery Tales from Around the World*
retold by Judy Sierra
(Houghton Mifflin)